SUPERHERO MUM

For Super-Susan-
Vanessa-Penelope-Shoe,
with love J.B.

To my
Superhero Mum,
with love T.K.

First published 2018 by Nosy Crow Ltd,
The Crow's Nest,
14 Baden Place, Crosby Row,
London SE1 1YW

ISBN 978 1 78800 022 2 (HB)
ISBN 978 1 78800 144 1 (PB)

www.nosycrow.com

Nosy Crow and associated logos are trademarks and/or registered trademarks of Nosy Crow Ltd.
Text © Timothy Knapman 2018
Illustrations © Joe Berger 2018

The right of Timothy Knapman to be identified as the author
of this work and of Joe Berger to be identified as the illustrator of this work has been asserted.

Printed in China
Papers used by Nosy Crow are made from wood grown in sustainable forests.

1 3 5 7 9 8 6 4 2 (HB)
1 3 5 7 9 8 6 4 2 (PB)

SUPERHERO MUM

TIMOTHY
KNAPMAN

illustrated by

JOE BERGER

nosy
crow

TOOLS

All mums are
truly **brilliant**
but sometimes
you'll find one . . .

who has a
special
something
– like my . . .

She gets up every morning
with a **superhero leap.**

Though sometimes
even **superheroes**
need a **bit** more sleep.

She does so many things at once,
she **ZOOMS** round everywhere –

mending . . .

mixing . . .

She must have **superstrength** because she carries **so much** stuff . . .

my scooter,
wellies,
coat,

and even that lot's not enough . . .

for when we have to **run**
because I see the bus drive by,
she picks **me** up and goes **so**
fast I think that she can **fly!**

BUS STOP

She makes up **super** things to do,
like this – my **favourite** game.

(And Monster Chasing Children
Round the Playground is its name.)

If I'm feeling sad or cross,
or when I've hurt my knee,
my mum's the **superhero**
that I **always** want to see.

As in a **flash,**
and with a **smile,**

my **supermum** appears,
with sticky plasters and a kiss,
to **chase away** my tears.

And when I'm playing in the bath,
she makes us both look **weird**
by giving each of us a
really **funny** bubble beard!

She **doesn't** wear a **cape**
or fly to Earth from **outer space**,
but she's the one who **saves** me
when there's trouble I must face.

Like sometimes, when I go to bed,
my teddy **isn't there**
and I **can't** sleep without him

SO THAT REALLY IS NOT **FAIR!**

My mum's the one
who **dashes** off

to have a look around . . .

in every nook . . .

and corner . . .

till . . .

I say, "You are my **superhero**, and the **best mum** too." She smiles and says, "Remember this, my love, because it's true . . ."

And then she holds me tight and **spins** me in a **super** whirl . . .

"EVERY mum's a

SUPERHERO

and so is EVERY

GIRL!"